Dear Parent:

Congratulations! Your child is taking the first steps on an exciting journey. The destination? Independent reading!

STEP INTO READING® will help your child get there. The program offers five steps to reading success. Each step includes fun stories and colorful art. There are also Step into Reading Sticker Books, Step into Reading Math Readers, Step into Reading Phonics Readers, Step into Reading Write-In Readers, and Step into Reading Phonics Boxed Sets—a complete literacy program with something to interest every child.

Learning to Read, Step by Step!

Ready to Read   Preschool–Kindergarten
• big type and easy words • rhyme and rhythm • picture clues
For children who know the alphabet and are eager to begin reading.

Reading with Help   Preschool–Grade 1
• basic vocabulary • short sentences • simple stories
For children who recognize familiar words and sound out new words with help.

Reading on Your Own   Grades 1–3
• engaging characters • easy-to-follow plots • popular topics
For children who are ready to read on their own.

Reading Paragraphs   Grades 2–3
• challenging vocabulary • short paragraphs • exciting stories
For newly independent readers who read simple sentences with confidence.

Ready for Chapters   Grades 2–4
• chapters • longer paragraphs • full-color art
For children who want to take the plunge into chapter books but still like colorful pictures.

STEP INTO READING® is designed to give every child a successful reading experience. The grade levels are only guides. Children can progress through the steps at their own speed, developing confidence in their reading, no matter what their grade.

Remember, a lifetime love of reading starts with a single step!

To my fourth-grade teacher, Ms. Gold
—M.M.-K.

Visit us on the Web!
StepIntoReading.com
www.randomhouse.com/kids

Educators and librarians, for a variety of teaching tools, visit us at
www.randomhouse.com/teachers

ISBN 978-0-7364-2778-4 (trade)
ISBN 978-0-7364-8093-2 (lib. bdg.)

Printed in the United States of America   10 9 8 7 6 5 4 3

Teachers' Pets

By Mary Man-Kong

Illustrated by Elisa Marrucchi

Random House New York

Chip learns to read.
Belle is his teacher.
She teaches Chip
the alphabet.

A is for apple.

B is for books.

C is for Chip!

Now Chip reads
to Belle.

He has fun!

Some fish take
a music class
with Ariel.

The fish play
the coral tubes.
They strum the
seaweed.

The fish blow
into pretty shells.
Sebastian and Flounder
dance to the music.

Ariel sings while her class plays. They all make beautiful music.

Tiana teaches kids
to make gumbo.
Tiana adds a pinch
of salt.

She adds a dash
of pepper.
Then a student
stirs the pot.

Tiana and her students
taste the gumbo.
It is yummy.

They share it
with their friends.

Cinderella teaches
Gus and Jaq to dance.

One, two, three.

One, two, three.

Gus and Jaq go
to a mouse ball.
They dance
the night away.

Cinderella is
very proud!

Rajah loves
to play games.
Jasmine teaches Rajah
to play hide-and-seek.

Rajah hides
behind a table.
Jasmine finds Rajah.

Now Jasmine hides
in a basket.

Rajah finds Jasmine.

Hide-and-seek is fun!

Aurora teaches
Buttercup tricks.
He jumps hurdles.

He trots in a circle.

The good fairies cheer!

Buttercup wins
the Royal Riding Contest!
He gets a ribbon.
He takes a bow.

The Dwarfs' house
is very messy.